JENNY'S JOURNEY

SHEILA WHITE SAMTON

SCHOLASTIC INC.

New York   Toronto   London   Auckland   Sydney

Copyright © 1991 by Sheila Samton.
All rights reserved. Published by Scholastic Inc., 555 Broadway,
New York, NY 10012, by arrangement with Viking Penguin,
a division of Penguin Books USA Inc.
Printed in the U.S.A.
ISBN 0-590-42526-9

8 9 10   08   10 09

This book is for
Willa Breslaw,
Janet Coleman,
and
Karen Wilkin

friends for a lifetime

One day Jenny got a letter
from her best friend
who had moved far away.
Jenny felt sad because
her friend was lonely.

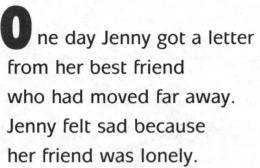

Jenny wrote back right away:

Dear Maria, I miss you too.

This is a picture of the boat I'll sail to visit you.

6

Here I come! The sun is rising and I'm setting out! I'm sailing my boat through the tugboats and the sailboats and the motorboats and the ferries,

8

"Where are
you going?"

and past the statue of
Our Lady of the Harbor,
and under a bridge,

till I get to the open sea!

Maria, I wake up all alone on the ocean!

Remember how lonely I felt when you moved away?
I feel lonely now, too, but then
a dolphin shoots out of the water.
Then another one! And here come some sea gulls!
They all want my breakfast!
It's like the day we fed the seals at the zoo.

I sail along. Suddenly I'm in
the shadow of a big, black wall!
It's an ocean liner! Far above
my head, a voice booms out.

"Little girl, little girl,
where are you going?"

"Don't worry,
don't worry.
I'm going to
visit Maria."

That night I steer my boat
through a chain of islands.

When I open my eyes
in the morning, *Oh, no!*
I'm caught in
a storm at sea!
The howling wind
fills my sail,
and all day long,
I steer up and down
waves like mountains,

until the ocean is calm again,
and I can take out
my guitar and sing.

"Oh, Maria, don't you cry for me,
for I'm comin' for to see ya,
right across the deep blue sea."

By now you probably think I'll never
get there. But the next day,

I finally see land!
There's a long pier
and *you* are on it,
waiting for me!

Hooray!

So don't feel lonely.
(And someday I really
will come to see you!)

Love, your friend,

Jenny